D1575094

Ocho Loved Flowers

Anne Fontaine

Illustrations by

Obadinah

My cat Ocho was crazy about flowers.

He loved to tug at the stems and chew.
"Ocho" means "eight" in Spanish.

Most of the time, Ocho was pretty busy.

Sometimes Ocho walked in a circle.

Around and around he would go, making his nest.

He liked to curl up on my bed.

Sometimes he made his nest on me!
Then Ocho closed his eyes and purred.
I liked putting my cheek on his fur.
Ocho was a soft, warm friend.

One day I looked for Ocho everywhere.

"Ocho! Ocho!" I called again and again.

At last I found him under the bed.

He made a strange sound.

He wasn't purring.

It wasn't his hungry sound, either.

"What's the matter, buddy?"

He made that sound again.

"Oh Ocho, I'm sorry you don't feel good."

I got down and very softly touched his fur.

In the morning we took Ocho to see Debbie.

Debbie's a vet.

She had to keep Ocho overnight.

She did tests to see why Ocho had a lump in his belly.

The next day Debbie met with us.

She said, "I'm sorry, Annie. I have bad news."

She said Ocho was not going to get well.

"How long?" said Mom.

"About thirty days," said Debbie.

"Thirty days for what?" I cried.

"Ocho is going to die, honey," said Mom.

My stomach felt terrible.

"No, not Ocho!"

I buried my face in Mom's soft coat.

In the car we didn't say a word.

There was only the sound of sniffles and tissues.

I kept my hand on Ocho's carrier.

Mom said, "We need to talk about how to take care of Ocho."

I sat down and started to cry.

Mom scooted next to me and gave me a hug.

"Ocho's my best friend. I don't want him to die!

Will it hurt him?" I said.

"Ocho will not be in pain.
Every day we'll give him medicine.
He may start eating less
and he may spend more time alone.
We can call Debbie anytime and she'll
come to our house.
That way Ocho can stay here with us."

"Can't they do surgery?" I asked.

"No honey," Mom said.
"Ocho's tumor is growing all through his
small intestine.
He probably wouldn't live through surgery."

"At least he'll be with us. We love him.
We'll take good care of him." I said.
"You bet we will," said Mom.
We petted Ocho together.

I stayed close to Ocho for the rest of the day.

Mom showed me how to give Ocho his medicine.

We wrapped Ocho in a towel. He looked like a burrito.

Only his head was showing. He squirmed.

"He hates it!" I said.

"It will help him feel better and live longer," said Mom.

I held Ocho's neck and he opened his mouth.

Squirt! In went the liquid.

"That wasn't so bad, was it, Ocho?" I said.

Ocho ran into my room and licked off the extra.

"Good going!" said Mom.

At the grocery store I asked,

"Can I bring Ocho some flowers?"

"Sure," said Mom. "That's a good idea."

I put the flowers in a vase and set them near his bowl.

He sniffed them. Then he tugged and chewed them.

Ocho was crazy about flowers.

Every week I got fresh flowers for Ocho.

I got him carnations.

I got him daisies and snapdragons.

Ocho ate less and less.

He slept more and more.

One day Debbie came over to check on Ocho.

I asked, "When is he going to die?"

"You'll know," she said. "He'll let you know."

I asked, "Will he just go to sleep and not wake up?"

"When he dies, he may look like he's asleep,

but he's not," said Debbie.

"Death means his body stops working.

After that, it won't work anymore."

On Tuesday Ocho wouldn't come out.

"Oh, Ocho," I said, "it's time, isn't it?"

I cried and hugged him gently.

I sat and petted Ocho for a long, long time.

"I love you, Ocho," I said.

Ocho became very still.

I kept petting him.

I could hear the birds outside.

I felt quiet inside.

You can say goodbye without words.

We buried Ocho that afternoon.

That night we went to Rudy's for hot chocolate.

Mom said, "Let's drink a toast to Ocho."

I said, "I loved how Ocho used to fluff up his tail

and snarl at the birds."

I raised my cup. "To Ocho!"

Mom said, "I loved the way you took care of Ocho."

"Thanks, Mom. I loved taking care of him."

I put away Ocho's toys in a box.

I didn't feel like playing with anything or anybody.

I missed Ocho.

For a long time I didn't feel hungry.

I missed my best friend.

One day I felt a little bit better.

Mom said, "Want to come with me to the store?"

"Okay," I said.

I walked right over to the flowers.

"Can I get two bunches?"

"Sure," said Mom.

I got one bunch for Mom and me.

I got another in memory of Ocho.

1. A veterinarian (vet) is a doctor who takes care of animals. Why couldn't the vet make Ocho get well?

2. Taking care of a cat or a dog is a big responsibility. What are some of the things you have to do to take care of a pet?

3. In the story Annie says, "You can say goodbye without words." What do you think she means?

4. Annie brought home flowers as a way to remember her cat, Ocho. What are some other ways to remember a pet or someone who has died?

5. What did Annie learn to do? Who did she learn from?